NONI the Christmas Reindeer

By Daphne Doward Hogstrom
Illustrated by June Goldsborough

CHECKERBOARD PRESS ❧ NEW YORK

Copyright © 1988, 1979 Checkerboard Press, a division of Macmillan, Inc.
All rights reserved. Printed in U.S.A.

CHECKERBOARD PRESS, JUNIOR ELF, and their respective logos
are trademarks of Macmillan, Inc.

Noni could fly faster and farther than any other reindeer at the North Pole, but she was never allowed to pull Santa's sleigh.

"You are too small," Santa told
her. "I need big, strong deer to haul
my heavy load. You stay home and
guard the stable, day by day."

But it was lonely guarding the reindeer stable every day. Most of the time, Dasher, Dancer, Prancer, Vixen, Comet, Cupid, Dunder and

Blitzen were off in the fields and
forests, running and jumping and
getting ready for their Christmas
Eve ride.

And, of course, on Christmas Eve
itself, they flew through the sky
with Santa's sack.

"Surely I can help Santa, too,"

thought Noni, one especially lonely
Christmas when even her friends,
the stable mice, had left her to sleep
together in the warm soft straw.

"If I cannot help *pull* Santa's
sleigh, then perhaps I can help
fill it!" she thought. "I will fly to
the farthest corners of the world

and find new and wonderful toys
for the girls and boys."

And, on the very first day after
Christmas, true to her word, off she
went to the four wide ends of the
earth!

"Good!" said Santa, when Noni found a little wooden clown that turned and tumbled, and stood upon his head in a hoop.

"Great!" said Santa, when she
found a tiny china chicken that
squawled and squawked and laid a
china egg.

"Grand!" said Santa, when she discovered a big silver robot—who walked and talked and stared with fiery eyes!

In the farthest nooks and crannies

of the world, Noni found more and
more wonderful toys.

"Marvelous!" said Santa, when a
queen in a faraway castle gave a
teddy bear that balanced on a string.

"Tremendous!" said Santa, when a prince in a far-distant kingdom gave a calico cat that swung upon a swing.

"Terrific!" cried Santa, when a king in a palace on a pinnacle gave a painted horse that pranced around a ring.

All year long, Noni found more and more toys for Santa's sack.

She found little tin trains that
puffed and whistled.

She found little tin planes that
flit and flew.

She found a fire truck with ever-

ready water, and a toy box with
ninety-five toys.

   She found paints made with colors
from the rainbow, and a book brushed
with stardust and dew.

She found a flute that played tunes forever, and a crystal ball that showed the sun and moon.

Finally, on a faraway mountain in a meadow—she found a magician making dolls that danced and sang!

"Perfect!" cried Santa at last, on Christmas Eve. "But my sack is filled to overflowing, so I'll need your help to guard my heavy load."

And, almost faster than Noni could fly—he hitched her up *behind* his waiting sleigh!

"Please watch out and warn for
falling toys," he called, as he
climbed to his seat beside the sack.
Dasher, Dancer, Prancer, Vixen,

Comet, Cupid, Dunder and Blitzen
flew happily at the front of Santa's
sleigh, steering their way through
the stars.

But Noni flew happily at the *back* of Santa's sleigh, watching for dolls that might tumble through the darkness, or for clowns that might topple through the clouds.

"I'll never be lonely again," she said—thinking of all the toys she would find for next Christmas, too!